This book belongs to

Tina Marie Smith

INDEX OF FIRST LINES

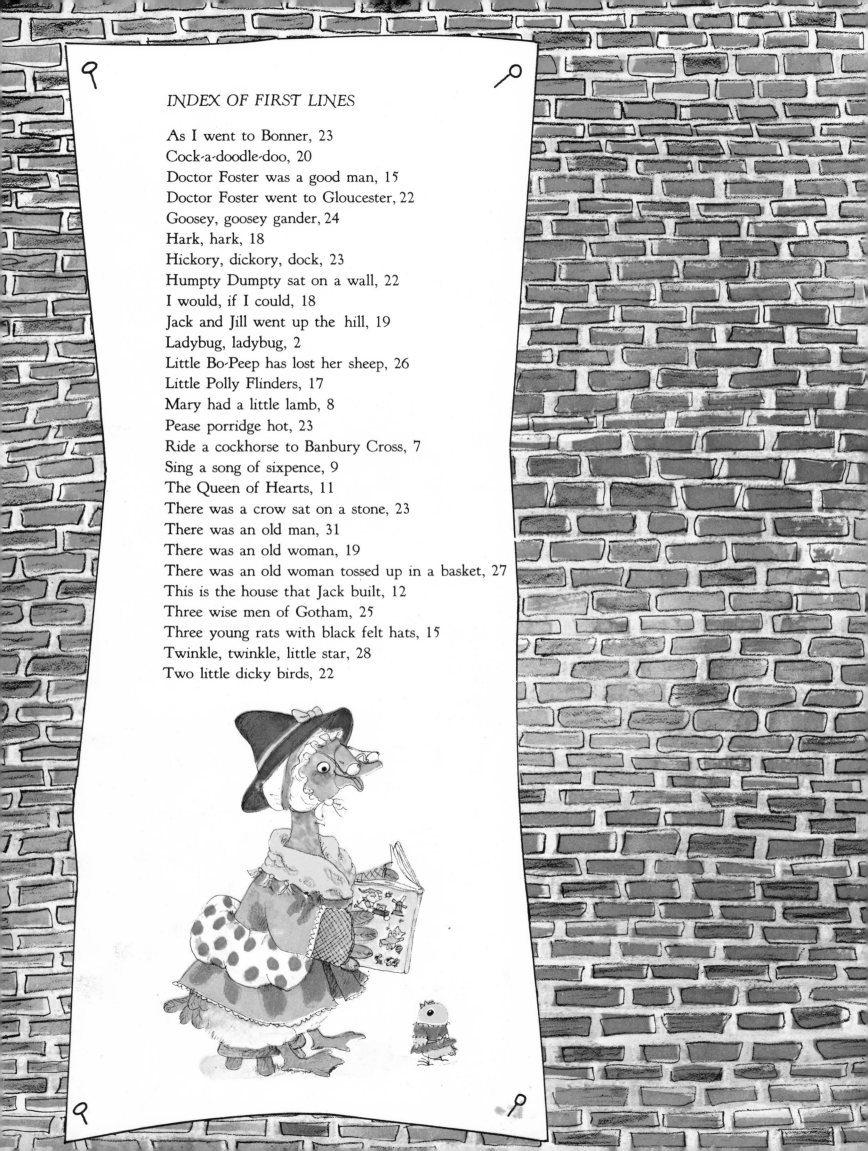

Richard Scarry's
Favorite
Mother
Goose
Rhymes

GOLDEN PRESS • NEW YORK

Western Publishing Company, Inc.
Racine, Wisconsin

Illustrations from RICHARD SCARRY'S
ANIMAL MOTHER GOOSE

1976 Edition

Ride a cockhorse to Banbury Cross,
To see a fine lady upon a white horse;
Rings on her fingers and bells on her toes,
And she shall have music wherever she goes.

Mary had a little lamb;
　　Its fleece was white as snow.
And everywhere that Mary went,
　　The lamb was sure to go.

It followed her to school one day,
　　Which was against the rule.
It made the children laugh and play
　　To see a lamb at school.

And so the teacher turned it out,
　　But still it lingered near
And waited patiently about
　　Till Mary did appear.

"Why does the lamb love Mary so?"
　　The eager children cry.
"Why, Mary loves the lamb, you know,"
　　The teacher did reply.

Sing a song of sixpence,
  A pocket full of rye;
Four and twenty blackbirds
  Baked in a pie!

When the pie was opened,
  The birds began to sing.
Was not that a dainty dish
  To set before the king?

The king was in his countinghouse,
  Counting out his money;
The queen was in the parlor,
  Eating bread and honey.

The maid was in the garden,
  Hanging out the clothes;
There came a little blackbird
  And snipped off her nose.

9

The Queen of Hearts,
She made some tarts,
All on a summer's day;
The Knave of Hearts,
He stole the tarts
And took them clean away.

The King of Hearts
Called for the tarts
And beat the Knave full sore;
The Knave of Hearts
Brought back the tarts
And vowed he'd steal no more.

This is the house that Jack built.

This is the malt
That lay in the house that Jack built.

This is the rat
That ate the malt
That lay in the house that Jack built.

This is the cat
That killed the rat
That ate the malt
That lay in the house
that Jack built.

This is the dog
That worried the cat
That killed the rat
That ate the malt
That lay in the house
that Jack built.

This is the cow with the crumpled horn,
That tossed the dog
That worried the cat
That killed the rat
That ate the malt
That lay in the house that Jack built.

This is the maiden all forlorn,
That milked the cow with the crumpled horn,
That tossed the dog
That worried the cat
That killed the rat
That ate the malt
That lay in the house that Jack built.

This is the man all tattered and torn,
That kissed the maiden all forlorn,
That milked the cow with the crumpled horn,
That tossed the dog
That worried the cat
That killed the rat
That ate the malt
That lay in the house that Jack built.

This is the priest all shaven and shorn,
That married the man
    all tattered and torn,
That kissed the maiden all forlorn,
That milked the cow
    with the crumpled horn,
That tossed the dog
That worried the cat
That killed the rat
That ate the malt
That lay in the house that Jack built.

This is the cock that crowed in the morn,
That waked the priest all shaven and shorn,
That married the man all tattered and torn,
That kissed the maiden all forlorn,
That milked the cow with the crumpled horn,
That tossed the dog
That worried the cat
That killed the rat
That ate the malt
That lay in the house that Jack built.

This is the farmer sowing his corn,
That kept the cock
    that crowed in the morn,
That waked the priest
    all shaven and shorn,
That married the man
    all tattered and torn,
That kissed the maiden all forlorn,
That milked the cow
    with the crumpled horn,
That tossed the dog
That worried the cat
That killed the rat
That ate the malt
That lay in the house
    that Jack built.

14

Three young rats with black felt hats,
Three young ducks with white straw flats,
Three young dogs with curling tails,
Three young cats with demi-veils,
Went out to walk with two young pigs
In satin vests and sorrel wigs.
But suddenly it chanced to rain
And so they all went home again.

Doctor Foster was a good man,
He whipped his scholars now and then;
When he whipped them he made them dance
Out of Scotland into France,
Out of France into Spain,
Over the hills and back again.

Little Polly Flinders
Sat among the cinders,
Warming her pretty little toes.
Her mother came and caught her
And whipped her little daughter
For spoiling her nice new clothes.

Hark, hark,
  The dogs do bark;
The beggars are coming to town.
  Some in rags,
  And some in tags,
And one in a velvet gown.

I would, if I could;
If I couldn't, how could I?
I couldn't, without I could, could I?
Could you, without you could? Could ye?
  Could ye? Could ye?
Could you, without you could? Could ye?

Jack and Jill went up the hill
  To fetch a pail of water.
Jack fell down and broke his crown,
  And Jill came tumbling after.

Up Jack got and home did trot,
  As fast as he could caper,
To old Dame Dob, who patched his nob
  With vinegar and brown paper.

There was an old woman
  Lived under a hill,
  And if she's not gone,
  She lives there still.

Cock-a-doodle-doo,
My dame has lost her shoe.
My master's lost his fiddling stick
And knows not what to do.

Cock-a-doodle-doo,
What is my dame to do?
Till master finds his fiddling stick,
She'll dance without her shoe.

Cock-a-doodle-doo,
My dame has found her shoe,
And master's found his fiddling stick.
Sing doodle-doodle-doo!

Cock-a-doodle-doo,
My dame will dance with you,
While master fiddles his fiddling stick
For dame and doodle-doo.

Two little dicky birds   Fly away, Peter!
Sitting on a wall,   Fly away, Paul!
One named Peter,   Come back, Peter!
The other named Paul.   Come back, Paul!

Humpty Dumpty sat on a wall;
Humpty Dumpty had a great fall.
   All the king's horses
   And all the king's men
Couldn't put Humpty together again.

Doctor Foster went to Gloucester
In a shower of rain.
He stepped in a puddle,
Right up to his middle,
And never went there again.

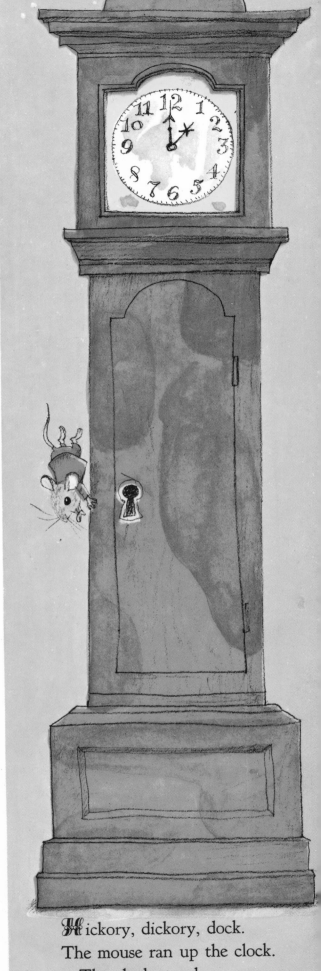

Pease porridge hot,
Pease porridge cold,
Pease porridge in the pot,
Nine days old.

Some like it hot,
Some like it cold,
Some like it in the pot,
Nine days old.

There was a crow sat on a stone;
When he was gone, then there was none.

As I went to Bonner,
I met a pig
Without a wig,
Upon my word and honor.

Hickory, dickory, dock.
The mouse ran up the clock.
The clock struck one;
The mouse ran down.
Hickory, dickory, dock.

Goosey, goosey gander,
Whither shall I wander?
Upstairs and downstairs
And in my lady's chamber.

Three wise men of Gotham,
They went to sea in a bowl.
If the bowl had been stronger,
My song had been longer.

Little Bo-Peep has lost her sheep
    And can't tell where to find them.
Leave them alone, and they'll come home
    And bring their tails behind them.

Little Bo-Peep fell fast asleep
    And dreamt she heard them bleating;
But when she awoke, she found it a joke,
    For they were still a-fleeting.

Then up she took her little crook,
    Determined for to find them.
She found them indeed, but it made her heart bleed,
    For they'd left their tails behind them.

It happened one day, as Bo-Peep did stray
    Into a meadow hard by;
There she espied their tails, side by side,
    All hung on a tree to dry.

She heaved a sigh, and wiped her eye,
    And over the hills went stump-o,
And tried what she could, as a shepherdess should,
    To tack each again to its rump-o.

There was an old woman tossed up in a basket,
　　Seventeen times as high as the moon.
Where she was going I couldn't but ask it,
　　For under her arm she carried a broom.
"Old woman, old woman, old woman," said I,
　　"Where are you going to, up so high?"
"To sweep the cobwebs out of the sky,
　　And I'll be with you by and by."

Twinkle, twinkle, little star,
How I wonder what you are!
Up above the world so high,
Like a diamond in the sky.

When the blazing sun is gone,
When he nothing shines upon,
Then you show your little light,
Twinkle, twinkle, all the night.

28